REAPERS
BY DANIELLA ROUCHY

INSTA;@daniella.g.m.rouchy

Daniella was born prematurely with many complications that required yearly operations, regular dental surgeries, and home recovery from birth to twelve years of age. During surgeries, she had turned to the comfort of creativity and imagination as she aged with each operation; all the surgeries stopped at the age of twelve as she finally settled with her family in England when her father retired from the army. Her passion to become an author increased throughout school and then college as her teachers admired her work and wanted her to continue towards her aim. She worked in and out of jobs when reaching eighteen. She wasn't able to get a simple job right away, not until being guided by job supporters and would gradually be introduced to volunteer work, then temporary and short part-time work. Even with the job complications and short-term work, she would always aspire to be an author. With little to no good grades, her confidence and willpower provided all she needed to be self-driven to success. Whether it was a new job or a new book, she would take any challenge and learn from each mistake and turn it into a learning curve. The only rule she lived by was very simple: have confidence in your abilities and in yourself. She took the confidence to not only write her stories with passion, but she even self-taught herself later on in life on all the skills she needed to edit and release each story, showing pride in each and every book.

PROLOGUE

To you, I am a omen.
To me, I am phantom.
To most, I am death…
I can see things that you can't, and it frustrates you, you try to piece what I am and how I come by, but that is my choice to decide, not yours.
A bus could come around the corner, and I can lead you to it, either to send you home, or to out-worldly gates called Heaven, Hell, Elysium, the underworlds, so many names for something that can't be of your hands.
My job is simple, I watch, observe, and listen to your every words and motions, if I feel you should be spared by the death today, a life shall be torn from me, so I only kill, I don't spare those when I know what the people have done. The targets are given to me, and I obey, and if I die, another shall take over, it won't end, it never will.
You must be wondering, why a monster like myself, explain what I do? It's simple, you just follow me, and I can show you.

Chapter one
MARTHA

"What part of adding more syrup don't you understand?", Denzel said with annoyance,
I said bitterly, "sorry, here how's this?", I ended up just taking the lid off the toffee syrup, and pouring the whole thing in the shitty customers to go mug.
Obviously, wasn't a good idea, but this guy, he just kept edging me to do it so I did, give him what he deserved.
Which ended up in me being fired.
Taylor, the manager, brought me into his office to talk over my forms, and just make the day end with a cherry on top.
His office was obnoxiously plain and looked like some sort of reception room. White squared walls, a deep brown carpeted floor, the dark grey locked drawers behind his

Soon an idea lit my eyes as I said enthusiastically, "I can fix it, I saw it on a crime show once, you just push it back in place, it can't be that hard",

she shooed my hands away from her face, only to say firmly, "no, we're not going to let you ruin my face more",

I gave a huff, only to move my hands to the door as I said reluctantly, "we'll go to the hospital then, it's not far from town",

Ava smiled gently as she joked, "that's been one of the best things you've said so far",

We left the washroom, and walked through the bustling town, heading to the open pathway next to the road to our left.

The large grass fields to our right stretched far, but started to drown in the mass of trees as the woods were closer to us, the further north we went from town, I hated this part of town, it can get dark at night, thankfully the council installed better lights, or we'd have a shittier day.

I glanced at Ava as I said shortly, "so what now? When we go to the hospital, what can we tell them?",

Ava had a sly smirk on her face as she didn't need to think about it, she said simply,

"that a hot-headed Latino decided to beat up not only a white girl, but a ginger too", we giggled at the joke, it lead me to sigh as I said in disbelief, "god he was a prick, I don't get how he got away with this, people like him, they should be struck by a car",

Ava snuffed as she said amused, "dark, but true.",

she glanced at me as she pointed, "hey, look at that, kitty",

I smirked as I looked left, seeing a black cat watching us from across the road, it was cute, and had shiny eyes. I loved how the sun brightens up their eyes.

I stopped as it was meowing, it had a fluffy coat, so it can't be a stray.

Ava soon stared at it, she wondered, "do you think it's lost?",

we watched the cat, seeing it patter its way to the edge of the road, only to sit down and watch us, and it meowed again.

I let a slight frown as I said unsure, "I don't know, but we can check back on it when we're done",

We slowly kept walking, seeing the cat stay put, it seemed to be enjoying the sun, laying down by the grass as the cars strayed past it.

As we kept going forward, we passed the bus stop that was a short walk from the hospital gates.

A man sat at the bus stop, he had a grey hood on, and matching jeans, along with white trainers. He had a dark black Doberman with him, it had an innocent look to it, watching us curiously, with its light brown eyes.

We gradually went past, heading to the opened hospital gates behind it.

The long wide pathway to the hospital was nice to see, so much better than seeing blue everywhere, that cafe just had too much blue.

Upon walking into the large squared hospital grounds, I glanced to my right pocket as I recalled, "I should probably tell my mum I'm fired, why don't you go in? I'll come in and join you after I make the call, we're not allowed phones on whilst we're in there",

Ava gave a soft smile, only to joke, "yeah, that's if you're still here by the end of the call",

I smirked, only to shake my head slightly, she knew my mum well.

As she headed into the building, I walked back down the pathway, strolling at a slow pace so I'm not near
the hospital, I stayed halfway down the path, far enough to not get told off, I'd rather not have more shit to deal with today.

Nervously I dialled the phone, only to hear

the beeping of the call going through, I walked further to the gate as the phone was crackling, I think the signal is bad here.

Thankfully the bus was parked by the stop, allowing me to get a better signal as my mum answered, "Martha, you're calling early",

I glanced to the bus stop, seeing the man still there as he waited for the line of people to leave the bus.

Gradually I said, "I'm fired, I can't just drag it out, I'm fired",

I walked outside the gates, going to the pathway near the main road.

My mum said sharply, "well, that isn't good, what the hell are you going to do now? Why did you get fired?",

my words stopped, seeing the cat again, he must have followed us, that's not normal for owned cats, it might be lost.

Shortly I stepped behind the bus, seeing the cat look distressed, it was trying to get across the road but it couldn't.

Ignoring my mum's words, I walked to the cat, only to hear a loud horn, lights blinding my eyes, and my body falling with harshness.

CHAPTER TWO
GRET

"You said it was fifty quid", I said with a frown, this girl is a joke.
Misty was growing up, and my little girl is now a haggling little bitch, just like her mum.
I gave a huff, seeing she wasn't going to step down as she said with a whiny tone, "Dad, come on, I just want to go out, and have fun with my friends",
we sat opposite one another in the dining room, it was in our small open kitchen. The kitchen was to her back, as mine was to the living room, hearing my football go to waste as I sat here trying to gain something from this, clearly not though, she always brings up the damn exams.
She said arguably, "well, do you think I've not earned it? I got an A in my last test, surely

that is to be rewarded",
I gave a grin, only to snuff her words, well, suppose she's not wrong.
I went through my wallet in a slight huff, considering I do my own business, you would think I'd carry less money on me, to stop this crap from happening every time.
My hands were still dirty from when I changed the plumbing at the old couple's place, and my dark black combat trouser and white vest was all murky and smothered in grease from that sink clog. Thankfully I have changed that many sewage pipes and sink pipes, I'm used to it.
I motioned her the cash as I said firmly, "fine, just take it",
She had a huge smile on her face, she looked all dolled up, and she was clearly going to be doing more than just going to town.
She had her dark black hair down, her lips painted bright red, she wore a tight black vest that had these weird straps that crossed over each other, and her shorts were above thigh height, she even had these long boots that went under her knees, she looked like a hooker.
As she got up to take the money, her shoes clanked as she said happily, "thank you. dad, I'll be back before twelve",

before she could take the money I tucked it towards my palm as she grasped the air, making a frown as I said seriously, "don't do anything stupid",

I gave her the cash, only for her to leave a red lipstick stain on my face, kissing my cheek as she said shortly, "don't worry, I'll text you when I'm on my way home, I'll call you if anything happens",

I gave a slight smile back to her, only to face opposite the table, looking at the empty chair as she left the house, shutting the door with a heavy thud.

I had my hands on the table, looking at my fingers as I muttered, "fuck it, already missed my game",

upon standing up, I heard my phone ring, Michael just doesn't know shit, why did I bother to hire him?

Gradually I picked the phone up as I walked around the table, heading to the fridge to the left side of the kitchen.

Shortly I had the phone in my right hand, answering, "the fuck is it now, Michael, I'm not working at the moment",

I opened the fridge, using my left shoulder to keep the door open as I grabbed a nice big can of cold beer, cracking it open with one hand.

Michael complained, "look man, I don't know how long I can keep working for you if you keep treating me like shit",
ignoring his words I said ruggedly, "what is it? A broken pipe, can't find the keys to the warehouse, even though we both have one. Come on mate, I just want to relax",
I took a nice gulp of beer as he explained, "Gret, we have someone in our fucking warehouse, alright? So you coming here or not?",
giving it little thought, I said with a huff, "fine",
I hung up the phone, leaving it on the countertop as I downed the rest of my beer, this better be worth it.
When leaving the house I took my car keys out, and sat on my quadbike, turning the ignition on after I put on my helmet.
Fortunately, I didn't live so far away from the warehouse, or the drink would have been left, but today it's just the day I don't care. If it's those pesky squatters again, I'm going to give them a well-earned shiner.
As the bike rumbled down the street, I went right, heading down the thinner roads to the industrial estate of the town, seeing Michael to the left side of the road, standing outside like a wet lemon.

He had his black overalls on, he had it unzipped, showing his murky white vest under it. His scruffy brown hair was swaying in the wind as I parked ahead of him, just an inch from running him over as I stopped harshly.

His face grew red as he yelled, "you shit-head, you could have killed me",

I hopped off, leaving my helmet on as I said with a grumble, "I didn't though, I need my meat for brain alive",

even though Michael was younger than me, he was more built, and he worked out a lot, but come on, how did he not want to deal with this alone? seeing a big broad guy should scare them off.

Michael had sweat down his dark skin, he seemed to be working on something out in the front yard, must have wanted to go back in but probably can't.

I went to the large warehouse door, seeing the shutters ahead.

This place used to be a plane strip back in the day, but the guy that had it left this place, and the council turned it into a factory ground.

Upon passing one of our cars, I went to the one on the right, taking out a long extended copper pipe, may not be much, but it can hurt if you get hit with it at least.

I held it in both hands as I questioned, "so is it locked then? Did they lock you out?",

He nodded only to state, "before you ask, I did try the back doors too, no point, all locked",

we turned left sharply, looking at my bike as a rattle could be heard, I didn't know what it was but it was too dark to see anything.

Michael said skittishly, "the hell was that?",

"it was probably something", I said unsure, but with a slight sarcasm to it.

Michael didn't look impressed by my uncertainty, but what else can I say to that? I don't fucking know what it was, could be a freaking demon for all I know, that demon being Michael's incompetence.

I gave a snuff only to approach the shutters, seeing the main door to the left side of it, this place was big enough to hide in, so I'm expecting a hunt.

Without hesitation I kicked the door, breaking the lock chain on the other side, it left an echo within the brightly lit warehouse, seeing the shelves, and long tables of pipes and gear for repairs.

I kept the bar in both hands as I said with an echo, "well, at least this time you weren't lying, someone is here",

As I said that, a pipe hit my face, thankfully I had my helmet on.

I dropped my bar, only to snatch the one from the woman.

She had scruffy dark black hair, light skin, and deep blue eyes, she looked young.

She seemed to be on something, I could tell from her sunken eyes and desperation to leave.

Michael went to my left as I said orderly, "shut the damn door",

He didn't say anything, but soon moved to the door as I barked, "now!",

as he went to the door, I kept the pipe firmly in one hand, taking my helmet off as I said annoyed, "you scuffed my fucking helmet, I hope that was worth it".

I took a better look at her, she had ripped jeans on, and a deep red hood with stains on it, she seemed to be homeless.

With franticness, she pleaded, "please, don't hit me, I can leave, I can go now",

I put the thick iron pipe to her chest, stopping her from moving as I dropped the helmet on the floor, letting it rumble as I said firmly, "you ain't going anywhere, if anything, I'll be going you a favour",

I went in my pocket, only to curse, "shit",

my phone wasn't in my pocket, I left it at home.

Michael started dialling as I urged, "call the pigs, get this one back in the pen",
the door slammed open, causing us all to look at it, seeing nothing was there, nothing but the wind that was progressing through the night.
I bit my lip, hearing the woman quiver as she said in a frenzy, "the eyes follow, it will follow, I need to go, I need to get out of here", she went into a panic, attempting to pry the pipe from my hands.
With a harsh push, I shoved her to the floor, only to mock, "she really is out of it",
I glanced back to Michael, seeing he wasn't there, he must be waiting for the police.
The wind was picking up, but I couldn't afford to let this disturbed woman out of my sight, she'd be better in a padded cell than out here.
I kept the bar towards her as she attempted to scatter backwards, she had tears flooding as she cried, "the monster is here, it's coming for me, I tried, I tried to cleanse and it didn't work, I came back to it",
a frown grew on my face as the lights flickered, I'm assuming a storm is on its way.
This isn't helping her calm down at all.
I glanced down, seeing her hands were bleeding, she was clawing at the floor as she kept going further into the room.

I slowly lowered the pipe as I calmed, "alright, crazy, I'm putting the pipe down, just calm the fuck down",

she watched as I cautiously put the pipe down, something I will regret, but her hysteria wasn't doing anyone any good.

She slowly went to stand up in sync with me. She watched behind me, growing paler as she said quiet words, she moved her mouth, but I didn't know what she was saying.

With haste she went for the table, grabbing an oil can, she held it as she said with shaken words, "don't come any closer, I will do it",

I frowned as I said confused, "do what? The hell you on woman?",

she started pouring the oil on herself, only to take out a lighter from her hoodie as she was in hysterics, she was trying to set herself alight.

She screamed as I fought the lighter with her, trying to get it off her as I gained oil on myself in the progress.

My hands were slippery, but I was too last, she was on fire, and her hands were burning, as was mine.

The pain of the fire started to intensify as I tried to pat it out, but it was just making it worse, it was passing

on the front of my clothes as I started to yell, "Michael, help me!",
my hands warmed, it was boiling, soon scorching as the woman was shrieking into her hands, she curled on the floor, echoing shrieks as I hurried outside, scrambling to the open door, and heading out into the windy grounds.

Michael wasn't anywhere to be seen, I didn't know where he went but I needed to think fast. I crawled upon the damp gravel of the front yard, digging my hands into it as I started to bury the front of my body into the wet mud under the gravel.

The burning was stopping, but the woman, her shrieks were stopping too, she was quiet.

My hands shook violently as I took them out of the gravel, feeling the grit touch the open wounds and under the skin. My vision was growing distorted as I looked up, hearing the patter of heavy rain progressing.

In all my life, I never thought to cry, but I just did, I forcefully cried, seeing two red glows ahead of me, they looked like cat eyes, it was strange, it was like a cat, but as it gained closer, I saw it was a car.

My body gave into my urges to sleep, laying in the sunken gravel and mud.

I thought the pain would go away, it only grew worse.

CHAPTER THREE
ENID

"you'll be fine", I said to myself in the mirror, this is stupid, it's just a meeting.

I looked at myself, seeing my blonde hair down, and my face lightly dressed in make-up, this interview got me dressed up, and for what? I may not even get it.

When sitting in the car, I glanced down at my light brown blazer and trousers, making sure everything was perfect, not a crinkle in sight.

I tapped on the wheel, looking right as I saw the building I needed to go in, it was a tall and pretentious work office, but I could make more money there than I can with my own attempt at an estate agency. It was failing, my self-business barely got me a house sold, so I may as well do one step at a time.

I let a huff as I shut off the car, opening the door as I left to head inside the building, seeing many people walk past me like I was them, or just didn't exist.

A security guard was outside the building, a big broad man, with pale skin, dark black hair, cleaned-up beard. He moved in my way as he said firmly, "ID please",
with a frown, I wondered, "Oh, I don't work here, I've got an interview",
he was sceptical, but he rung inside, using his phone as I was ignored until he was ready to talk to me.
He gave a slight nod, only to hang the phone up as he informed, "sorry we can't have you in, you're late",
I looked to my left wrist, checking my watch, and seeing the time bright as day, I showed him it as I said sharply, "I'm ten minutes early, I don't think you understand",
he cut in, "no entry",
As he said that, dozens of people were just walking past him like this wasn't even happening.
I scoffed as I said with disbelief, "fuck that, I'm going inside",
he stopped me from entering, putting his hand to me as he pushed me away from the door, making me bump into this guy.
The guy was slim, dark, and well-dressed, he had a dark grey suit on with a white shirt under it. He looked middle-aged but seem to care well for himself. He gently stopped me

from falling as he said, "stupid drunks",
unintentionally I blurted, "you fucking prick",
I glanced to the security, seeing he now had more of a reason to not let me in.
The guy walked off, and I yelled, "that's okay, you let him sabotage my interview",
my hands soon started to shake as I was panicking, I never had this happen before, the hell is wrong with these people?
My voice shook as I said angrily, "you better let me into this god-damn interview, I was on time, I was early",
the guard just smirked as he showed me his phone, seeing it was five past four as he remarked, "you're late, now go",
my anger turned into desperation as I pleaded, "I don't have a job, I just got fired from my last one, please just let me have this chance",
the guard was quiet, he didn't say a single word, he was waiting for me to leave him alone.
Angrily I took my high heels off, throwing them at the guard, which resulted in a window smashing into pieces. The window to his right was shattered, allowing me to see the large hall inside as the guard yelled, "you now have the police on you for property damage",
god, fucking damn it, nothing is going right recently, things just keep getting worse.

Seeing that things can't get worse, I said loudly, "you and your fucking corporation can go fuck yourselves", I showed him two middle fingers as I backed away from the building, only to hurry to my car as he wasn't kidding, I was gonna get called in for this.

As I turned the car on, the guard hurried over, trying to stop me before I drove away from the property, heading to the outskirts of the town, I may not be able to out beat the police, but damn it I'm not giving him the satisfaction of him seeing my arrest.

I kept driving until I saw the road that lead to the bridge past the motorway, it was only one for pedestrians, so I went on foot. I ditched the car to the side of the road.

Before leaving, I opened the glove box to the left side of the car, taking out a whiskey bottle as I said annoyed, "today is the day then. Good thing I didn't ditch all my drink in the sink",

I was in rehab for a few months for my drinking issues, that was until now, fuck it, it's already bad, I might as well add to it.

I walked to the left side of the road, walking on the pathways that went through the trees to my left. As I gradually walked down the long pathway, I opened the bottle, smelling the strong scent of whiskey, and it stung my nose.

I took a drink, only to pull a face as I said choking, "forgot how strong this is", I started coughing, only to pull myself together, forcing more drink in me as I walked further into the woods.

I didn't eat anything all day, the nerves got the better of me, but who cares, the world is stupid, and this whole fucking dream of mine is nothing but dog shit.

When drinking more I glanced around, seeing the spring tree leaves blow around me, it was almost therapeutic.

A sigh left me as I drank half the whiskey, feeling tipsy as I muttered, "just drop the drink, get a job, that estate shit doesn't work. Well you're right Jordan, you were fucking right",

my other half wanted better for me, and even though he said it with harsh words, it was true, I could have made him proud of me for once today.

My eyes followed the dizzying floor, seeing blurry streaks of green as I passed the leaves, seeing the mud stick to my feet as I forgot I threw my shoes, well what use would they be anyways?

Gradually I glanced ahead, seeing a back blur on the pathway, I couldn't make out what it was, but I walked straight through it, must

have been some
shadow. My head was spinning, nothing was clear at the moment, but it was something that let me go.

The light grey bridge was just ahead, I could tell by the cars that sounded ahead, it was a nice walk on a long day, even though my house was far away from this point, I just liked to go out, find a place to look at and just zone out.

My feet started to trip on something, probably myself, I did go through the whole bottle. Suddenly I fell to the floor, smashing the whisky bottle against the bridge's concrete floor.

The shatter rung in my ears as I grumbled, forcing myself off the floor, not feeling the glass that dug into my hand as I said with a sigh, "shit, well that's not good",

when crouching on the floor, I heard a cat, it was weird, maybe I drank too much. I glanced up, seeing a black cat approach me, it was fluffy and had really orange eyes, it was curious to me as I wondered its way towards me.

I meowed again, making me scrunch my face as I sighed, "seems like someone noticed me today", as I went to pet it, I heard a man call, "you alright ma'am?",

I looked back at him, only to return to the cat, which no longer was there.

Gradually I got up, using the bridge rail to support myself, my hands shivered as I used everything I had to get off the floor. I felt light, everything was moving around me, and the floor was wobbling as I stood there, looking at this policeman who had someone with him.

They had yellow vests on, their uniform was official, and the guard certainly called them on me.

My left hand stayed hold of the rail as I said loudly, "I'm not okay actually, but for your sake, I'll just", my words got stuck, and my throat felt weird.

Quickly a rush of vomit hit the floor as I hurled over, making a mess on my feet and bridge as I threw up. The police were gaining closer to me with caution as I wiped my face with my jacket, only to take it off as I said, "shit, my jacket",

the police lady with him said cautiously, "why don't you step away from the rail, let us help you out",

I glanced left, only to say slurred, "I'm

assuming you were called because of a shitty security guard, he didn't let me in, I could have gotten a job today, but no, I had to stay out here",

they stayed put as the man didn't make another step, they were a good few feet from me.

Blood was dripping from my hand as I showed them the cuts, I said annoyed, "this shit, wouldn't have happened if they let me in for my god-damn interview",

the man said softly, "why don't you come to us, alright? We can see about this interview",

I snuffed, they don't give a shit, they're lying to me.

I climbed the rails, having my back to the traffic as I said upset, "you don't even see me, you don't care, you just say what you want to say and that's it, you're the fucking heroes",

the lady said something to the guy, unsure of what to do as I held the bars, the blood was making it harder to grip, but I'm making a point, a dangerous one, they don't care. No one does.

I said in bursts of tears, "I only went for this shitty interview cause no one believes in me, no one thinks I can do it. My partner is a lowlife fuck that wants me to get money for him, the security guard sabotaged me", the glass that was in my hands started to tear into my hand, making it bleed more as it was growing harder to hold onto the rails.

The policeman hurried to me, to which I let go, letting my body fall to the floor, hitting a car as it pushed me to my right.

I landed on my right side, facing the edge of the road, hearing cars suddenly stop as I stared aimlessly at the bushes on the other side of the road.

I feared to move, I don't know if I was alive or not, but I could see still, I was breathing still.

The cat I saw from before, was staring back at me, it meowed to me, only to prance towards me in a fast stride. It had glowing orange eyes this time, it made me frown, only to shed tears and mutter words as it was to my right hand, it gave it small nibbles, only to lick it as it started to make its way to my chest.

Gradually, it started to sit down, curling itself into my arms as my eyes shut, hearing it purr calmly as the darkness shrouded me.

CHAPTER FOUR
REAPER

The dangers of ghosts, the dangers of people's choices, I can't help but feel bad for people who don't know what to do, what there is to do, it's simple.

My job won't be to tear people apart, its to take them when the time comes, if I see you, it's your time to choose, your choice to make me like you more, or make me hate you and ensure you die a painful death if I can help it happen.

I lurk when you are close to that time, or maybe when you are already dying, I watch, but I can't save you, I would lose a life, I can only spare so many, and for me, my time is on my last.

The person I see who is dying, I can comfort them if I like them enough, or I can just watch you scream bloody murder, death happens for a reason, some may be unjust, and that person who killed you may very well be dead in prison, or I might just scare them into an oncoming train.

Let me tell you something though, those who kill, will have their turn, everyone does, even if it's unfair that you didn't fight back, know that I was watching, I will kill them inside out, puzzle in their minds to create a world they despise, and simply by a click of a gun, a drop of the rope, or a screech of a car, they will go away for good, and their graves will not be mourned, but know yours will be.

My time lurking on Earth for a thousand years has brought me to where I am, overly attached to those who see me for what I am. Drawn in history as the plague, a god of death, but the simple thing to this is that some humans deserved my pity, and they went on to do great things.

What made me save them you ask?

Their heart was in pain, and they were outcasted from the world, people wanted them to be like the rest, normal, and have achievable goals, what's achievable about drowning in a world of repetition? You work and earn that money, for it to be taken from you, unlike me, you can just go to a rodent and eat it, and live under the homes of those who see the world their kingdom.

I say outcasts are what add shadows to the bright world, we create a big enough one to show them what we can do, and how big our goals are, and we make it happen. But unfortunately, most humans don't dream so big, it's a shame, and makes watching their demise less pleasurable.

They have fear in their eyes, they plead, they cry, they know they haven't done anything with their lives, or not heart their hearts cry their dreams. Yet those who have done the dreams, cry still, but in their eyes, they know they settled with life, they have done what they wanted, and for that, I tend to reward them with a second chance.

There was one person, however, I spared, they did nothing with their life. They were just a child, but still, even a child says they have dreams, they tell you what they love, and this one child, they wanted to die, they dreamt dreams of abuse, they were moved from home to home, sold for cruel intent. I watched her stare at me, she was lying on the road in the dark, waiting for a car to pass over her on the motorway.

She watched me approach when a lorry was on its way towards her, she didn't show fear, but I feared she was to do great things, she just needed someone to care, so I did.

I sat near her, sniffing her hand, smelling the scent of her aura, she was roses, she was only a young teen, she going to not be a child and become a teenager. I glanced to the lorry, only to roll inside her arms, letting her hold me as the lorry was to intercept us. I show as a shadow near other eyes, to help protect myself from outsiders, but she would have seen the true me.

The lorry killed me, but the girl was under the lorry, just barely unharmed as I ensured she would survive with what injuries were to come with it.

She went on to become a voice for people like her, she told me in her stories as a shadow of hope, and luck was on her side.

I dwell on my sacrifices, it reminds me to be careful about who I spare, as one person that I spared, only went on to kill those who they did not know, creating madness and just more bodies in the dirt.

We are called the Reapers, we sow ourselves into the grounds of the earth to deliver people to the underworld, the dirt that decides where you shall go.

Our forms can be in many shapes and forms, I am unfortunately a cat, but that means I can be more agile, some of my acquaintances are dogs, and some are wild animals, we all depict many forms to either helpcomfort a dying soul, or scare the crap out of people who are to be killed, you'd be surprised to how many people are afraid of cats.

We have many intentions, our jobs though are very simple, it's following those near death, seeing if they live it out, or helping to give them a push when the time is near.

One person that needed to go on my list, was very lucky, the man was a drug dealer, and he had his running with the gang he was against, he had many younger kids killed for his job, getting no blood on his hands, so I kindly delivered blood to his doorstep.

His foe had listened to me, we agreed it was time for him to go, so one night, he went into his home and killed him in a very bloodied way. The guy had used a knife to kill him, making sure he was stabbed for every kid he had used against his gang, it was a lot of stabs I tell you, but sometimes, deaths can be just, you just need the right tool with the perfect puppet behind it.

Reapers can be your worst nightmare, but sometimes they can save you without killing themselves, we save people all the time, most people call it instinct, or luck, but all they do is watch us, and take our warning. It all comes down to when we look into your eyes, your strength and determination may save you, or your desperation may just lock the doors forever.

In my time of deep thinking, I walked down the long roads, passing by hedgehogs that had perished, hoping to burst the tires of the cars that would run them over. Their shadows would wander the roads, unable to leave as their bodies will never be at rest, one of the hedgehogs has been here for years since I was delegated to this town, and I grew to like him a little.

He would wander to my left as cars would pass through us, and he liked to stay to my left as I would stay to the far right side of the road, as much as I liked the cars passing through me, it was distracting me from our conversations.

I called the hedgehog Odious, he thought it was after Odin.

No, it was because his corpse looked repulsive, when I saw it, it looked like a flattened bit of paper, spikes everywhere, blood was staining around him, and eyes popping out, I shudder at the thought.

Odious was pattering away on the road, his spikes looked all nice, as though he was never run over, his nose was twitching to every car, and his beady eyes would look to the floor, wondering where his body was.

His mouth wiggled as he said shortly, "why can't you just, not kill people? Isn't that part of your job?",

My soft voice spoke, "because I'm not death, just his servant. I only scare people to their deaths, or I manipulate most to do the job for me",

As my feet pattered, I glanced ahead to the bridge I would always pass, only to stop as Odious wondered, "well, they ran me over, can I kill them?",

I saw this lady, she was very upset, almost rung a note in the heartstrings as I stated, "you don't need my permission, you're a ghost, do what you want",

I gradually pattered my feet to the right side of the road, seeing the hill that lead to the top of the bridge as Odious stayed behind, waiting to puncture a tire.

The pathway to the bridge was steep, but I found the way when seeing this abandoned car to where the pathway started, they had stopped the car down the main road we were just on, and she walked to the bridge, hmm, this will be an interesting watch.

CHAPER FIVE
GRET

Weeks passed since that shit show, don't know who that woman was, but I was going to find out either way. She had spoken about this thing, the eyes of the sun, or whatever she was on about, words of a madwoman if you ask me, but can a mad woman show that much fear for something of her imagination? She was scared of something, and now I fear it too.

Michael was missing also, they said he had rung up the station, told them what was going on, and he just left his phone, no other words after that.

My daughter even went missing on the day, shit was downhill, and things were out of my control. She was a smart girl, not a stupid fool, she couldn't have succumbed to some idiot boy, I sure hope not.

Thinking of the day, I went to my old workshop, seeing it was back to its normal state like nothing had happened, I still kept my business going, but I kept the links small enough so I could scrape by, I have things to find out, I have a daughter to find.

I had my warm clothes on, I had jeans and a thick grey jumper under my dirty blue overalls, my rough brown boots still had scuff marks from the fire, and my hands were also still recovering from that shit show.

They had me this burn cream when in intensive care, which worked a dream, but my hands, looked like wrinkled pups, the scars were healing, yet my fingers needed to move, so they adapted to wrinkles to accommodate movement.

I looked at my hands, seeing the frosty gravel under my feet, I turned the back of the hands to face me as I sighed. I thought of the woman, I tried to stop her but she didn't give up on her death wish.

The warehouse creaked ahead of me, telling me to go down my spiral of despair, which I'll continue to do so until I find my little girl, and find my best friend, Michael may have seen me as a bully, but I was doing him a favour, toughen him up a bit, but maybe I was too tough.

With another huff I entered the building, hearing the scene of the fire playback as I approached the room, shutting the door behind me as I locked it shut.

I trailed my way to the table, hearing the woman's cries as she warned me of those eyes, I think I saw it on the day, but I don't think the monster was anything but a car, so maybe not.

Upon leaning on the table, I had newspapers scattered over it, looking for this monster the woman spoke of, was she scared of a killer? There have been murderers and a lot of suicides in this godforsaken town, but nothing linked, I searched on her, she has no relatives, she was an orphan.

I had the town map pinned to the table, having the newspapers to the left side of it, as my many coffee cups were to the right of the map, I should really bin them, but I need to focus.

To the north of town was where my daughter went, she was at her friend's house, and a house party went wrong, but all the people there said it was close friends, not strangers, and they turned an eye for a second and she was gone, they couldn't have predicted this to happen, but I sure as hell did.

I pinned the house with a green pin, seeing as

that was her favourite colour, and with Michael, I pinned his red, he liked red. My warehouse was southeast to the town map, she was far from me, and I don't think she could be anywhere in town, I searched every inch of this place.

My thoughts trailed as I said out loud, "so you were here last, I've already searched the woods, maybe I didn't search hard enough",

I glanced right, hearing my phone go off in my pocket.

Cautiously I picked up the phone and answered, "this is Gret, what do you want?",

A woman answered on the other side, she was in hysterics, she pleaded, "help me, they have me, they want me dead",

I frowned as I worried, "Misty? The hell, where are you",

the phone went dead, I looked at my screen, seeing it was dark as though the phone wasn't even on at all. I clicked the power button, seeing the call had ended, this was strange, where was she?

I slammed my phone on the table, having a deep breath as I cursed, "shit, shit",

whoever has her, they want me to find her, and I sure will, I just need to show this to the police and they can track it, they have to track it.

As I took my phone, I put it in my pocket, hastily leaving the warehouse as I hopped onto my quad bike.

Upon driving to the police station, just west of the shopping centre, I sped faster at the thought of Misty being in trouble, she needed my help.

My thoughts froze when harshly breaking, seeing this guy walk out, he was in a grey hooded jacket, and he just glanced at me and kept walking, not like this isn't a fucking crossing, idiot. I glared at him through my helmet, not as he will see it, but he surely will know.

I slowly kept driving down the enclosed street of homes, making a left turn to the shopping centre road, passing the bustle of people. Christmas lights were being set up, the community people were setting them up, it was nice to see people ignoring two missing people, can't believe this.

Gradually I met with the police station ahead to the left of the shopping centre, the building was small, it was a halfway point, a temporary stay for some until they were passed onto a bigger prison.

With swiftness I parked ahead of the building, looking to the window to see people were inside, some officers were there too, one specifically behind the desk looked like they were bored out of their mind. When getting off the bike, I took my helmet off, leaving it tied to the bike, trusting no one will steal it in front of the police cameras outside, if they do, they're stupid.

When entering the bright white reception room, I could see the officer behind the desk to my right, she was in full uniform, tapping away on the computer. There was a row of five chairs to the left side of the room, watching the opposite side of the room as people entered and left behind her, there was a double door to her right, which people were being escorted to, some in handcuffs, some not.

I noticed there was a dial phone to the left side of the room, near the chairs, no change was needed, the only thoughtful thing the police have done. They acted like this case with my daughter, Michael and that woman was nothing to worry about.

I looked ahead, and seeing a pin board that faced the door, I approached it, seeing if they had my daughter up there, or Michael, it was a missing person board.

The policewoman watched me as I approached the board, looking for Misty as I wondered, "why is she not on here yet?",

The woman glanced at me as she questioned, "can I help you with anything?",

I glanced back to the board when I turned to her, I stated, "yeah, I had a call earlier from this woman, she was in hysterics, I didn't know if you could track it, make sure this isn't some prank call",

The lady seemed intrigued as she took the phone, she wondered,

"when did the call happen?",

thinking back on it I stated, "a few minutes ago, not that long, I had to drive up here from the south of town if that helps",

she glanced to me, only to put the phone in the bag as she said shortly, "we'll get a better look at it, it won't take long, why don't you grab a seat, and I'll get someone to help you",

she gave a slight warm smile, only to enter the double doors, she had a weird tone to her, I couldn't place my finger on it, but perhaps she was sincere, hard to know what that sounds like.

As I looked at the chair, I glanced right, seeing the pin-board, maybe they just didn't have enough room for all the missing people, but that doesn't make it right for Misty and Michael to not be on there.

My attention went to the phone, hearing it ring, I looked to the desk, seeing the officer wasn't back, maybe I can pass the call on, or just keep the person on the line.

I approached the phone, and picked it up as I answered, "hello?",

the woman was on the other side, she was in hysteria as she said, "help me, the eyes of the sun, they want me dead",

I frowned as I called to the desk, "hey!? the lady is on the phone",

I don't know if they could hear me, but I needed to keep this lady on the phone, I soon responded, "we need to know where you are, where are you?",

I dropped the phone, letting it hang as my hand started to feel like it was burning, the woman was screaming so loud, she sounded in a lot of pain. A policeman accompanied the officer I spoke with earlier, they were alert as I cupped my hand stating, "the phone, 'there's someone on it, she's the one I was talking about",

the lady went to me as she took a look at my hands, seeing the scars as she questioned, "are you hurt? Are you burns irritated?",

the man went to the phone, only to pick the phone up with ease.

He had it to his ear, listening to the woman as I looked back to the officer, she prompted,

"do you need to sit down for a bit? I can get a

medic to look at the burn scars, make sure you're alright",
with a frown I stated, "no, no I'm fine. Look, I just need to know where that woman is, on the phone, she just rang up here, she must have access to some sort of landline too",
the man hung the phone up as he ensured, "don't worry, she'll be fine, we'll get your hands looked at, and you can be on your way",
Confused I challenged,
"fine? She sounded like she was screaming bloody murder",
the lady rephrased, "he means we'll get someone to her location, if it's on a landline, she should be very easy to spot",
I glanced back to her as I wondered, "you have my phone, if you know where the woman is, can I have it back then?",
the man stated, "what does it look like?",
he walked to the desk, seeing my phone behind it as he stated, "this one? Here, you have it back, I'm sure we have enough to run by",
I faced him as I stated, "why haven't you found my daughter yet? ",
slowly he gave me my phone, giving me a strange look as he said, "who's your daughter? I can look it up on the system",
the policewoman stated, "Misty is still on the

missing person list, but we'll find her, I'm sure of it",
I glanced at her, taking in her comfort before saying,
"just keep me in the loop if anything shows up on her",
I turned back to the man, only to depart from the station, heading back on the quad bike and going back to the warehouse, trying to gain clarity on what this woman was.
She had used a landline, so maybe I can stop by the library, and find out if there's a landline plan to the city, they must have something I can look through to pinpoint her location.

Chapter Six
Carter

I waited in the hospital ward for Martha, she was in a bad way, well I was told anyways.
Ava sat with me, her nose was bruised but she said she was fine, the doctors told her it was just a beating, nothing broken at the very least. She was to my right, tapping away at her phone as she worried, "I can't just keep holding off on what to say",
I pointed, "well you've been typing and deleting for the past half hour, just say she's in a bad way, that's what we are told, but they're doing what they can to help her out",
Ava again deleted her text, making Martha's mum wait longer to what is going on.
With a sigh, I suggested, "just ring her up, the people are watching us you know, you can't have your phone on in here",

she glanced around, looking to the right side of the open hall, seeing this reception lady watching us occasionally, she was back to her work when she saw Ava make eye contact with her.

Ava gradually stood up as she nudged, "can you get a coffee then? I'm sick of looking at that cafe",

I smirked, looking opposite the room to the cafe and eating lounge.

We were in the hospital for a good few days, and it became a week, thankfully, Martha was fine, it was just to go with her to her x-rays, and make the progress reports before two weeks later she was all clear on the checks.

We left the hospital, walking down the pathway as Martha, Ava, and I headed to the bus stop, making a left to go down town.

Martha looked opposite the bus stop, making a double take across the road as she wondered, "did you guys see that?",

We stopped with her and stood by the bus stop a few people waited out, only two hooded chavs from the looks of it, but they were talking to one another, smoking, and not taking notice of us.

I glanced at Martha when seeing to what she was looking at, it was just the woods, nothing much, but this-place will always make her jumpy, she did get run over so it's understandable.

Ava gently put her hand on Martha's shoulder, she encouraged, "come on, let's go, take out isn't gonna order itself",

I gave a slight smile to her, only to motion Martha to join us, she was gonna be skittish for a while.

Martha was to the inside of the pathway, away from the road, we made sure of it as I stay to the outer side, walking a calm pace as I thought out loud, "so what are you guys getting? Pizza, Indian, oh, or maybe some Mexican food, I do love a good quesadilla",

Ava smirked as she said curiously, "sounds like you may want to join us",

Martha added, "you can join us for dinner, even though it's a girl's sleepover, sure you can stay for dinner",

I gave a smile as I said happily, "great, thankfully I don't have a curfew. Did you want me to order the food from my app, and get it to your house a few minutes after we get there?",

Ava shook her head only to state, "nah, we can order it when we get there, have you around a little longer",

We had a nice walk through town, Ava didn't live too far from it, making it easier to get to her home, it was a house just to the east of town, near the main road, thankfully, it was a quiet day as it was working hours, so not many cars were driving around three to two o'clock, or Martha would be having an anxiety attack.

We walked to the row of homes that faced the town behind us, seeing the two-story semi-detached houses to our left and right, they were cream colour, it was recently built to gain more people to our town. Martha was more at ease seeing the Christmas lights up on Ava's home, the street was dotted with them but Ava went out more with it, she had an inflatable Santa to the right side of the home, seeing it was near a road, it stood out more as no houses were in the way of its view.

Ava had a smile as she crossed the road ahead of us, she was eager to show us what she was doing in her spare time. She had her back to her house, having her arms wide out as he said loudly, "welcome to the north pole",

Martha smirked as she wondered, "I don't see any penguins or polar bears",

As we crossed the road, Ava sorted her dark green bomber jacket, putting the sleeves down as she stated, "well, there's humans on it, so yeah, close enough",

I laughed, she wasn't wrong.

Martha had her causal wear on today, a white shirt, blue jeans, red converse, and a red and white bomber jacket to match it, she was meant to be at work, but they gave her the day off due to the nature of her hospital appointment, she forgot to tell them the date, and she let them know last minute, but thankfully, she found a better place to work in. She stood ahead of the gates to Ava's front yard, standing in admiration of the small square lawn as she wondered, "so, you still have this place? thought after with Taylor, you'd be kicked out",

Ava smirked as she stated, "I had two jobs, secret agent work", Ava pulled her fingers to look like a gun as she pointed at different angles, being silly as she make shooting sounds before blowing the tips of her fingers.

We laughed at her joke, only for her to go to the front door as she stated, "the new job is better full-time, I just like you guys so I stayed",

As we trailed behind her, Martha smiled as she joked, "it cost you a nose though, and some pride",

Ava turned back to us as she opened the door, putting the back of her hand to her forehead as she said dramatically, "a price I had to pay",

She laughed at her joke, letting us enter the tight corridor as she motioned, you guys go in the living room, I'll join in a minute",

We passed the stairs to our left, going right as we entered the open living room and kitchen.

Her flat-screen TV was mounted to the wall facing the stairs behind us, the large fluffy brown sofa stared at it as we passed it.

We didn't think to take our shoes off, but they weren't that dirty, and Ava didn't mind.

The dark oak coffee table was ahead of us as we sat down on the sofa, Martha was still in pain from the accident, but the doctors said all she needed was painkillers for two more weeks, and the rest of it is just the body doing its job, I'm glad she didn't get hurt so badly.

Ava joined as she shut the door behind her, she went to the kitchen on our left, she offered, "tea?",

Martha said shortly, "yeah please",

"Sure, can you make it strong?", I said curiously, Ava was to the counters spread to the left side of the room, her feet tapping away on the light white marble tiles as she went from one side of the kitchen to the next.

She switched on the dark black kettle, she looked at me unsure, she said with uncertainty, "Well, I just make tea, didn't realise there was a strength volume to it",

I chuckled only to accept, "I'll just take any tea then",

Martha looked at me as she wondered, "you still work for Taylor? See you're in normal clothes, not his blue",

I was wearing my dark grey jumper, and dark green joggers and matched it with a dark green jacket with white stripes down the arms, I said with a smirk,

"after seeing you two coming out like from Carrie, thought it was time to beat it too",

with a smile, I added, "yeah I left him for good, he was a dick.",

Ava stood with her arms crossed, listening to us as she had her back to the counter, letting the kettle boil as she questioned, "you said you work in town, but where? I didn't think to ask you fully",

I looked at her as I answered, "that sports shop, the one where they do a mix of clothing and gear for it, the Sports Centre, pretty cool, I get a twenty percent discount working there, I get paid on the weekly",

Ava moved from the side, pointing at my clothes as she motioned, "ash, that's why you look like a rich chav today",

I smirked at her remark, only to look at Martha as she said sincerely, "thank you, for leaving Taylor's Cafe, you didn't have to", with a warm smile, I said briefly, "well, I got a better wage, a better boss, and my friends don't work there anymore, why would I want to stay there? at least now we can get a fresh start",

Martha smiled warmly at me, only to recall, "oh, we should get dinner, I'm starving",

She took her phone out, already placing the order as I prompted, "I can order, this is meant to be your treat",

She waved her hand a little as she reassured, "it's fine",

as Martha started to type the order in, clicking options on her phone, she asked, "so you wanted a chicken quesadilla?",

I gave a nod when adding, "do they do sides too? I'd like rice with that",

She added it as she ensured, "make that three, sure we can feast after the weeks we had",

Ava smiled as she gave us our tea, putting it on the table on top of these slate stone cup coasters.

Martha soon wondered, "what did you want Ava? Fajitas?",

"hell yeah, you know me too well", Ava said enthusiastically.

Dinner was ordered and we talked for ages, it was nice to not be so tense all the time, we were all worried Martha may have worse injuries, well, the doctors said she was in a bad way anyways, maybe they were surprised it wasn't as bad as it looked.

It reached around half-five when I decide it may be time for me to leave the girls to it, but we stayed out in her front lawn a bit before separating ways.

Martha had her hands tucked under her arms as Ava did the same, I zipped up my jacket as I stated, "I can go now, it's fine, you two seem like you'll turn into ice blocks out here",

I smirked a little, it was dark out here, but Ava's home was a glory of light, it was like a kid's dream of what Santa's home would look like.

Ava shook her head a little as she stated, "no, we just like to stay cold, besides, we thought to wait for your ride to come, sure taking a while though",

Oh, that's why they were staying out here.

I laughed at her words, only to explain, "no one is picking me up, I'm gonna walk home",

she snuffed as she refused, "no, not with how this town is lately, you hear the news? a lot of people popping",

Martha said quietly, "Ava",

"Sorry, you know what I mean though, it's not safe out here, not even for a macho man like Carter",

I glanced at my pocket as I stated, "can't call my room-mates, they're out for the week, and I don't; think my dad would appreciate me calling him up to drop me off, especially since I don't live with them anymore",

they saw my point, but it was late, even if it was five o'clock, it was nighttime virtually with this winter weather.

Martha said suggestively, "well, maybe get a taxi then",

I soon stated, "No cash on me, look, I can just stay on the phone with one of you guys if that's what you're worried about",

they seemed to be at ease with that idea, it wasn't a long walk I had to do either, it was to the west of town, not far, a half-hour walk at least.

Martha and Ava hugged me at the same time, doing our group hug goodbye before I left for town, passing through the bright lights and bustling streets, hearing people chatter away as I called Ava's phone, hearing it ring.

She picked up as she said, "hello, who's this?",

I pulled a face as I said sarcastically, "just the landlord, you're evicted",

we gave a laugh, only for her to wonder, "so hows is your room sharing going?",

I walked straight ahead, going through the

underpasses that went under the roads of the town, not caring about the dim lights under them as I stated, "well, it's okay, they're barely there half the time, so its nice, I get loads of space",

Something felt weird when I glanced back, I saw this cat walking behind me, it was dark black with red eyes, it must be from the lights of the under tunnel.

I smirked as I cut in on myself, "aw, you would love to see who I just saw",

happily, she said with a gasp, "is it a cat?",

I stopped halfway into the tunnel, having my back to the end as I faced it, seeing it walk towards me with a little jingle of its collar.

Gradually it stopped ahead of me as I said to Ava "can you hear its collar? It's pretty cute",

She couldn't hear it so I crouched to the cat, putting my hand towards it, but it just stared at me, it might be cautious.

I started making noises to get it to go to me, it stood up and meowed at me, only to run off as it hissed at something behind me.

With a frown, I stood up and said, "damn, never mind Ava, it ran off",

Upon turning around I bumped into this guy, dropping my phone as I apologised, "sorry, sorry I didn't see you there",

He picked my phone up, only to hand it to me as he said stiffly, "careful boy, people will want this",

the guy was wearing a dark tracksuit, he had a pale rough looking face and looked like a gangster, but he seemed fine, it's not about the looks as they say.

I took the phone, only to have it to my ear as I thanked, "sorry again, thank you",

he gave a nod, allowing me to pass him as he walked away.

Ava worried, "what happened? Are you okay? Who the fuck was that?",

shortly I reassured, "it was a guy, I just bumped into, I didn't see him, it's fine, chill",

Gradually I stopped walking, seeing a few more guys ahead of me, they seemed fine, but they didn't move, well this is the time for those types of people to be out.

One of them had a dog, he was far from the others, but it was odd, I couldn't tell what dog it was, but it was skinny, and seems to have pointed ears.

The people looked at me as I whispered, "I'm in the second under past west of town, I'm going to have to hang up",

The guys looked at me as one called, "oi mate, your phone working bruv?",

I hung up the phone and hesitantly said, "yeah

man, do you need to call someone up?",
In this situation, be their friend, well if you can help it anyways, I just need to get past and I'm all good. The dog started growling when I got closer to them, only to viciously bark as one of them took my phone.
The people took no notice of the dog as they chuckled, "yo who's Ava? She your girl mate?",
I went to take my phone back, but the taller guy pushed me as he said, "you starting on us?",
They laughed with them, they were in light green to red and blue tracksuits and seemed to be good with their money.
My heart tensed as I got up, only to state, "I'll just go the other way, it's fine",
I again bumped into the same guy, he seemed to be the ring leader as he pulled a knife to my throat, he said ruggedly, "don't think so kid",
my hands stayed in his view, only for him to look to the tall guy as he motioned, "kill the lights, start from
the end, make your way here, I want this to last",
my eyes locked onto his with fear as he pinned me to the tunnel wall, the dog was still barking loudly, pulling closer to me as the man in the dark tracksuit had him held back.

The man looked to be middle-aged, he was older than the rest who were hounding around me as the man said, "posh lad, where did you get this tracksuit from",
Smartly I said, "think you already know",
put his arm to my neck, choking me as he said with his teeth gritted, "don't be a smart ass",
the lights in the tunnel were getting darker, the tall guy was slowly going to each one, letting his feet drag as he chuckled at the man's words.
The man put his hand to my throat, only to balanced the knife to the side of my face as he said, "listen here, you take off your clothes, and give them to me, we may leave you alone, but you don't listen to me, bad things will happen kid",
the dog's growl was gaining closer to me, he stood to the man's left, letting me see its menacing amber eyes as the guy was cut between the group.
It snarled as I said, "come on, it's cold man",
He hit the side of my face, letting me fall to the floor, seeing the light above me as the dog was moments from my face.
Its teeth were snarling and its angry eyes looked down at me as the guy was on me, he had his feet to my sides as he said darkly,
"that's fine, I did warn you bad things will

happen",

I screamed with horror as the lights were out, and the man-made stabs at me, as the dog barked and snarled before its eyes turned a glowing yellow, making me see its gnashing teeth before it attacked me.

I kept my eyes shut, it was dark, and I was cold.

I'm cold.

Chapter Seven
AVA

"Carter? You there still?",
I looked at my phone, seeing he had hung up, this wasn't good at all.
I stood up as I huffed, "Martha, we may need to go out and get Carter",
she stood up with me as I hurried into the kitchen to get a skinny LED key ring torch, it was tiny but pretty bright.
Martha worried, "did he say where he was? What's going on?",
as we hurried out of my house, I didn't think to lock up, there was no time, I just shut the door firmly as I stated, "Carter said he's to the west of town in the underpass, he just stated he was there and hung up",
we paced our way through the street, going through town, ignoring the people as I started to dial the police as I Martha urged, "we

should call the police",
when ringing them we were by the underpass, hearing a commotion as I stated, "take the phone, I'll run them off",
Martha whispered, "what the fuck, you can't just go in there",
I turned the light on, only to head through the underpass as I staged, "stop right there. We're going to need back up",
I shone the light so it was in their eyes, not being able to see me as they scattered, believing I was the police, I don't care if I get told off for faking a cop, Carter was in trouble. The people left with haste, abandoning the underpass as I approached Carter, seeing his bloodied body on the floor, my skin went pale when seeing the stab wounds on his stomach.
I yelled back, "call the ambulance, he's bleeding badly",
I put the torch on the floor, hastily taking my jacket off and putting it over his stomach, as though it would stop the blood from leaking from him.
Martha raced down as she said, "they're coming here, what state is he in?",
she looked over my shoulder, she looked like she was going to throw up as she reported, "he's bleeding badly, you need to hurry",
I said firmly, "he's breathing just barely, we

may just have got here in time",
my hands were in a tremor as I put pressure on the stab wounds, containing the injuries until help arrived. It was a cold night, no doubt he will be cold on this floor, goddammit, he should have just stayed with us.
Martha snuffled as she said, "shit, its that thing again, the hell is it doing?",
I didn't know what she was talking about, I stayed focused on Carter as I stated "come on, we can't lose our heads now",
she crouched to me as she put the phone to her chest, she motioned, "look, it's ahead of us, that's what I saw, it was the cat, you know it",
cautiously I looked opposite us, seeing a glowing pair of eyes, it didn't look like a cat.
I kept eye contact with it as I said with nervousness, "the fuck is that, that not the cat", my hands were urging me to let go, but I stayed put as I said briefly, "we need to stop the bleeding Martha",
I glanced at her as I snapped again "Martha", I let her stay close to my left as I stated, "you put your hands there, I'll go the other side",
I kept watch of the eyes, seeing it was glaring from afar, but it did edge closer by a little.
My breaths were short but I kept focused, we need to keep Carter stable for the emergency

services, they have to be here soon, it feels like it's been ages.

With haste I put my hands on the other side of Carter, keeping the pressure on him as Martha left the phone on speaker, she put it to her left as the lady on the other side asked, "are you still there miss?",

Martha said with a shaken voice, "yeah, yeah, just hurry, how long?",

The lady said patiently, "they're in town as we speak, how is Carter? Is he breathing",

Martha glanced behind me, she was frozen by her words, but I kept her hands put on Carter as I stated, "he's breathing at least, but he has lost a lot of blood",

she glanced at my hands, seeing one was on hers to keep her in focus, I know the thing was watching, I could feel its breaths were behind me, but I can't shake off the feeling that it's not here, not truly, it's watching, that's all I was worried about.

I looked ahead of me, looking past Martha as I said happily,

"they're here, Carter, they're here",

Martha looked behind her, seeing the paramedics and police on their way to us.

The medics approached and one questioned, "what's happened?",

he crouched to us as I stated, "he's been

stabbed, I don't know how long ago, he's still breathing though",

The medics took over as the policeman took us away from the scene, letting us go to the edge of town where they had parked.

I looked at my hands within the blue flashing lights around us, so much blood, I didn't realise how bad we looked until we were in better lighting.

We were kept in the police van, out of public view as they got us cleaned up, well, our hands anyways, don't think we can change clothes.

We sat on the right side of the van, facing opposite the two policemen as they handed us wipes as one said, "it's alright now ladies, your friend is in good hands",

the brown-haired man to my right had a notebook, getting a good grasp on the times as I showed them my phone, letting them know I had him stay on the phone with us until he got home.

The man handed me my phone back as he asked, "did you see the people that attack Carter?",

Martha gently shook her head, she was in a bad place, she's been through a lot as it is.

I took it upon myself to answer the questions as I stated, "we saw a gang, but they ran off

when I shone the light on them, I scared them away, and they thought I was a cop",
He gave a sly smile as he ensured, "smart, don't worry, you won't get charged for impersonating an officer, say it was a white lie",
I said shortly, "you can track them down, can't you?",
as the man shut his notebook, he ensured, "we have cameras down in that area, so we have a start at the very least",
Martha jumped when she heard a knock on the door, I gave a slight hold of her leg to reassure her it was fine. She glanced at me, seeing the person on the other side of the door was one of the paramedics.
They popped in to have a look over us, no doubt we have trauma, but who wouldn't have trauma after witnessing that?
The woman sat with the policeman, as the blonde-haired one left the van, giving us extra space, and also checking up on Carter.
We got checked over and got offered to get some counselling to just talk about what we saw, I didn't need it, I was staying strong for Carter,
that and the fact I was already in counselling therapy for my past issues with my parent's nasty abusive relationship I was tied in, so

yeah, that explains why I didn't give a shit about that weird thing in the underpass, I don't even know what that was.

Martha and I were given the all-clear to go home, they had dropped us off at my place, which now gave me a less cheery feeling than earlier, but I was glad to be home again.

When entering the house, I let Martha in first as I stated, "I'll get the kettle on, you can get some of my Pyjamas on, bin these clothes, I don't think the blood will come off so easily",

she headed upstairs as I locked the door behind us.

I walked to the kitchen, turning the kettle on as I sighed, I rubbed my face as I was still computing what happened earlier, poor Carter, I hope he pulls through.

As I finished making us tea, Martha came downstairs with one of my fluffy grey Pyjamas on, she seemed to be calmer as she went to the left side of the kitchen, throwing her clothes in there as she said with a sigh, "there go my good clothes",

she let a smirk as I said softly, "Carter was always a messy person",

her smile faded to upset as she started to tear up, I took off my blooded jacket before hurrying to comfort her, I hugged her as I hushed softly, "he'll be okay, he has to be okay",

I was a little taller than Martha, making her have her tuck her head under my chin as she said solemnly, "there was so much blood Ava, I don't think he's okay",

With a slight smile to myself, I said shortly, "there's no harm in hoping",

she said with a sigh, "yeah, suppose you're right",

I let her move away first, allowing her to compose herself as I said briefly, "I'm gonna get change out of these, did you want to get a film on?",

I looked at my phone as I stated further, "it's nearing half six",

even though she wanted to say no, she wiped her eyes as she said, "you get changed, and I'll think about it",

As I left the room, heading upstairs to my bedroom on the far right side of the hall, Martha sat on the sofa, sitting with her cup of hot tea as she stared at the blank TV.

I got changed into some fluffy black Pyjamas, hurrying downstairs to make sure she was still okay, to which I slowed down halfway when seeing her sitting on the sofa still, I was worried she would run out to Carter, but we just need to wait, they said they'll call us when he's in recovery.

Hence why I suggested watching a film to make the time pass quicker.

She glanced at me as I walked behind her, going to the kitchen with my bloodied clothes, putting them in the bin as I questioned, "so, did you want to watch a film?",

she sipped on her tea as I walked towards her with mine, sitting to her left as she said curiously, "I saw you have the Pluto console, that's meant to be the best console they have", The Pluto console was pretty good, it was a rounded ball console, and no discs were needed as the games could be downloaded digitally.

I put my tea on the side when turning the TV on, and took the two controllers to form the TV unit, the controllers were pretty awesome. It was a V shape, you held both sides, there were two analogue sticks to the top part of it, the back buttons behind it, the arrows were to the left under the left stick, as the right stick had four round buttons under it, they were flat buttons build into the controller, making it smooth, like a touch screen almost. Lastly, the power button was at the bottom of the controller in the centre, making it easier to turn the console on without getting up.

As I showed her how to hold the controller, I listed, "I have some good games on it, one is a two-player shooter called Zombie Grave, doesn't make sense in the name, they don't stay in the grave, but it's a full-on shooter round game",

Martha looked unsure as she questioned, "maybe something less, gory? think I'm all good with the blood today. Any puzzle games?",

I looked to the purple screen that showed up, seeing my duck icon pop up with my name under it, as I clicked it I showed her the games I had.

We finally settled on a two-player puzzle game, which was Ducktective Two, the first one was amazing, that's where I got my free duck avatar from. The game was about a chick that becomes a detective, and searches for its family, its mum, it had a dark back story for something so bright and cute, but either way, Martha had a smile on her face seeing the cute carton ducks standing around in a two-dimensional interrogation room.

We have a long night ahead of us.

Chapter Eight
GRET

"I know, I just need updates, I came into the police station earlier",
The police lady I saw earlier, Lara, rang up to give me details, but they have a lead on what happened to her, and where she went.
I was with my new apprentice, Memphis, he was a good lass.
He was broad and tan, and he had worn his overalls with the arms around his waist, so it would show his vest.
He was standing by the table, looking at my mini-crime board, not really sure what to call it, but it's all I have of my little girl, and I was surely finding her.
Lara ensured, "we'll do what we can, we'll keep you posted",
I glanced to the dark phone screen, seeing my tired eyes as I sighed.

I looked to Memphis as he said shortly, "nothing back yet?",
I gave a slight shake of the head, only to reassure, "sure we'll get somewhere",
When putting my phone on the table, having the screen down, Memphis wondered, "so, what do we do now?",
I glanced at the open door to the front yard, seeing the un-worked van as I stated, "we should fix up the van, it only needs new brakes, and just a bit of TLC",
he gave a smirk as he ensured, "sure thing boss, we'll get this done today, no problems",
I didn't mind the new guy, he showed up quite suddenly, but it's just another member, Michael isn't being replaced.
When stepping out into the cold grounds, I looked at the van, it was a bit frosty, but it will be fine to work on.
Memphis was a sit-back-and-wait guy, but that's due to not knowing if I needed help or not, and in all fairness, I liked getting my hands dirty, so for the moment, he was my lackey, until I felt he could be trusted.
When working on the first set of breaks, I heard someone call my name, I kept working, but they said it again, to which I slid from under the car.

I saw the neighbouring warehouse owner, she was a pretty red-headed fox, with blue eyes, and glasses, and seemed to take care of herself well.

She gave a wave from the gate, not wanting to come too close for some reason.

Shortly, I wiped my hands on my overalls, seeing the break oil wasn't coming off so easily. Kate gave another smile as I said curiously, "hey Kate, sorry for the mess, you can come in if you want, I can get Memphis to make a brew for us",

I glanced back to the open door to the warehouse, she glanced past me, only looking at her sleek blue jeans, white jumper, and brown boots as she stated, "I best not, I have to pop into work, oil stains everything",

a gentle laugh came from her, only to stop abruptly as she wondered, "I was just popping by, to see if you're doing okay",

my body shivered a little at the words, for some reason it just felt weird for someone to be asking if I'm doing okay.

My throat felt the words grow stuck, she slightly stepped towards me as I said honestly, "not well, I miss her, I miss Michael",

her words grew soft as she invited, "well, if you need to talk about anything, I'm a phone call away, or down the road",

She pointed to her right, pointing to the large grey warehouse down the road. Her company was a delivery storage unit.

Kate stood in a moment of deliberation, she wanted to move closer but she stopped herself, she just said sweetly, "I'll stop by after work, we can go for a coffee",

I let a smile, only to see her leave, it made me feel warm seeing she cared so much.

When going back to the van, I saw a shadow from inside, I couldn't make out what it was. Gradually I entered the warehouse, and saw Memphis by the table, he had the coffee on the table, it looked to be cold though. I let a smirk when approaching him, I picked up the cup as I pointed, "no steam, this is cold",

he motioned to the door as he remarked, "not my fault, you were busy talking to your little bird",

with a shake of my head, I let his comment slide.

I drank the cold coffee, not bothered by it, I enjoyed seeing Memphis look in disgust though, the only reason I would ever drink cold coffee, it would be nice to have a hot one with Kate later.

The day was long, with a lot of back and forward, but we finally got the van fixed, you can press the brakes on it at least, however, it wasn't quite road legal just yet.

The last part of the day was to lock up the shop, but I lived here after what happened with Misty and Michael.

I didn't really get a lot of sleep, so I must look like a zombie to others, yet as far as I can tell, I don't give a shit what people think about me. Even though it was dark, Memphis walked home, he didn't seem to mind the dark, but I still said for him to get in touch if something feels off, this town isn't as safe as it used to be.

I went home before leaving for town, getting out of my dirty clothes and into something casual, but a little on the dress-up side to impress Kate.

Misty bought me this really nice fur jacket a few months back for my birthday, I wore that, with a white shirt, along with dark rough jeans, and deep brown boots.

I took my quadbike to town, using the free parking, then waited around in the bustle of town for Kate. It was only four in the afternoon, but it felt later within the winter period.

Upon sitting on a bench, I stared at the towns central statue, it was a giant cat standing on a rock, along with a dog to the left of it, and a snake to the right, the statue never made sense to me, but it looked oddly welcoming when people looked at it. The snake was coiled below the rock, the dog was standing next to the left of the rock, and the cat was gazing at the sky, looking at the stars that were showing.

I never really went out much, but the statue, I never thought to read the plaque, after years of being here.

I glanced at my phone, seeing Kate's message ping, she messaged, "five minutes away, awful traffic",

I let out a slight smile, only to look back at the statue again.

Gradually I approached it, observing the plaque as it faced at an upward angle. I soon read quietly, "To when curious, the adventure can shudder, bravery can stride, though fear can show. Show it no mind, and fear will wander. Though show it fear, and your mind will go to ether.",

it wasn't signed off, it looked to be a community art project.

Kate startled me as she said, "pretty cool art piece isn't it?",

I glanced to my right, seeing her smile widely, she was closer to me, now that no oil was on me. Gradually I stated, "seems a bit, odd if you ask me. Cat, Dog, and then a snake, what does this even mean?",

We stood a little further away from the statue, Kate seemed to enjoy the question as she said in thought, "it was inspired by life, the cat is the compass to curiosity, and the dog is protective, but to whom?",

she gave a smirk, seeing I wasn't getting it, but she still went on, "the snake is like the anchor that keeps things still, hence why it's holding the stone, not the animals",

I gave a glance to her, only to admit, "Okay, that is pretty cool to know", I soon pried, "though you know too much about this bronze lump",

Kate nudged her head behind us, getting us to stroll away from the statue, as she said, "because I helped set it up, I may own a delivery company, but we do have some good tools to help. I then started to ask the people who were with us, they had the whole class there, and a mix of people and clubs made this.",

gradually, she gently brushed my fingers, giving me a signal, if I wanted to hold her hand or not, it gave a blush to my face, but I kept my cool.

She slowly locked fingers with mine, holding my hand as she said briefly, "Gret, I'm
worried for you, I had a call from a policeman

earlier, saying you just barged in the station, demanding Misty's whereabouts",

I thought this date was more of a pry session, but I suppose she dens;t know the full story.

We strolled through town at a slow pace, seeing the shops to our left and right, from sports shops to food shops, it was nice to see something different.

Shortly I stated, "the police, they haven't told me anything, Misty, and Michael, they're gone, what else can I do?",

she paused a moment, standing where she was stood as she said softly, "it's never easy, no one has it easy, not even the police when it comes to Michael and Misty",

gradually, she pulled me, holding both my hands.

Her blue eyes looked deeply into mine, making my heart go into heavy thumps, as though it was trying to feel something more, it was hurting so much, and get it pushed itself to fix me again.

She gently kissed me, holding it for longer as she put her hands to my face, even if I was taller than her by a foot, she tiptoed to accommodate the height difference.

A smile held my lips, as our lips parted, she stood on the floor normally as she said

gradually, "you look like you could do with

more than a coffee, why don't we get some pub food and a drink or two",
happily, I said, "could do with some food",
she giggled softly, only to move to my right again, looking arms with mine as we went to the Hunters bar, a great place for food.
Didn't think I would end the day dating Kate, after the long days in the warehouse, it gave me anxiety to leave it alone, but Kate relaxed me a little.

Chapter Nine
Martha

We visited Carter again, we made sure we saw him after work, even when he said it was fine, we couldn't let him recover alone for a lot of the days, especially to what I saw that day. Something was odd about it, I saw this cat thing, it had orange eyes, looked like it was going to come for us if the ambulance crew didn't get to us first.

Ava and I sat next to Carter, to his left, watching over him as he slept still, the machine kept him in a coma, he was beaten really badly when we found him.

I glanced around the small white room, seeing nothing but walls, a window behind me, next to where the door to the hallway was, it felt dead here, I didn't like hospitals. I looked to Ava as I wondered, "what do you think will happen now? The police said they're on it, its been four days already, no word of anything, my parents don't have anything else to say apart from 'they'll find them, don't worry', I highly doubt it at this rate",

Ava glanced to Carter as said firmly, "we will find them if they don't, Carter is on the mend at least, they said they'll bring him out the coma in two days, not long at all",

I gave a slow nod, only to think back on the night, I stared at the monitor as I questioned, "you saw it too didn't you?",

Ava was fixed on Carter, staying silent briefly, gradually she said shortly, "yeah, but I don't know what it is",

I got up from the chair, not believing her, she followed me as I stated "bullshit, you know what it was, you told me to ignore it, how stupid do you think I am?",

Ava glanced to Carter as she expressed, "okay yeah I know what it is, but we need to talk about it out the room, he can hear us, I don't want him getting worried",

I looked to him only to answer firmly, "sure he will be fine, he'll probably want to know too",

she let a slight exhale, she tugged on her black bomber jacket as she explained, "I saw something like that when I was a kid, playing at an abandoned park, it followed me, didn't seem to do anything when I ignored it",

I listened intently as she went on, "I couldn't tell what it was, it was too dark, but the eyes changed when I climbed this water slide, it was bigger, looked like dogs eyes or something, it just watched me, it barked at one point, nearly making me fall off the fucking thing.",

With a frown I glanced to the monitor, seeing it was spiking weirdly, I stopped Ava as I worried, "Carter, his thing is going weird",

I hurried to him, letting Ava get a nurse as I tried to calm him down, I held his hand, giving him brief comfort.

His hand tightened, causing him to gasp for air as he sat up in a mass of panic.

Carter's eyes darted around as I urged, "calm down it's just me",

sweat dripped from his face as he clutched his stomach, seeing he was in no condition to even sit up. I helped him back to his pillow, laying him down as Ava hurried into the room with the nurse, they were both shocked to see him awake, I think talking about the glowing eyes woke him up.

The nurse looked over his wounds as Ava and I were outside with a doctor, they wanted to know what happened, which I gave them the sugar coated version, he woke up due from us talking about the event, not anything in specifics, don't think I want them thinking we're crazy seeing orange glowing eyes.

Carter was stabilising, but we were told not to mention the event so soon, or again until he wants to, which is more than fair, we didn't plan for him to wake up in such a panic state, or at all.

Ava grabbed us a tea in the take out cups, at least we could chill for a bit before having to leave, at least gain something about what had happened, we did follow to what the nurses said and to not mention anything, but Carter was more talking about it than we were.

He mentioned he didn't know the guys, there were a gang of them, one of the guys bumped into him twice, he was the ring leader, but other than that, they were described as the simple chav gang, which was no help to us to find out who did that to him.

Yet he said about the glowing eyes, he said he was more terrified of that than the guys, which was odd but it was unnatural.

We sat on the bench near the window of the hospital, looking outside occasionally, as though we were being watched.

Ava expressed, "there's nothing we can do about these things, they just show up when they want to",

I stressed, "you saw what happened to Carter, what it did to him, what else are we going to do?",

she shifted a little, giving a glance to the window as she didn't k now what to say, or she just kept it to herself as she sipped her tea, thinking of what we can do, now that we know all of us saw the same thing.

Ava gradually put the cup down as she ensured, "I don't know what we can do, but we'll find a way", she was going to say more but a yell stopped us, it was this guy, he looked like in early forties.

He wore a white shit, dark jeans and brown boots, think he was the mechanic at the back of town, everyone knew him after what happened to Misty.

The guy looked around as he said with annoyance, "I got a call to say she was here, you can't stop me from seeing her",

I glanced to Ava as she whispered, "we should go, rather not be in the middle of this",

I agreed, the guy has gone a bit haywire since the whole ordeal with his daughter, I felt bad for him, he needs help.

Cautiously we took our cups as he went on a rant, talking about this lady who was on drugs, the warehouse burned down and how she was here, he wanted answers for something.

The guy looked to us as I gave him a glance, he stopped me in my tracks as he barked, "hey, I know you, you're the one that got hit by the car by the bus stop",

Ava looked to me as she gently took my hand as she redirected the attention, "you got the wrong woman, we don't know what you're talking about",

It didn't convince him, but he just watched us leave, he seemed to understand he was making a scene, but something in his eyes screamed desperation as I looked back to him, he was looking for something.

As we left we finally could breathe, Ava slowly let go of my hand as I said shortly, "thank you, I didn't know what to say to him", she gave a slight smile as she reassured, "no worries, he seemed to be lost, looking for something he can't find",

I think we're also lost, we're both on the same page of finding something that isn't there, but I don't know what to say, what can be done about the answers we seek.

We strayed down the hospital pathway, looking at the bus stop past the gate as I said briefly, "I think we should talk to him, if he doesn't get arrested",

Ava shook her head, she said firmly, "no,

that's a bad idea. He needs to figure it out on his own, I know it's harsh but we can't help him, he has to help himself",

In some way she was right, but what can a blind man see?

In the thought I drank more of my drink, only to stare ahead, seeing that damn cat again, it was weird, this time I crossed the road without worry.

Ava watched as I said shortly, "I think we should talk to him",

I looked to the hospital, seeing the cat ran inside when the guy stormed out.

She was going to argue with me but soon looked to the guy as she huffed, "guess we have no choice now",

the guy softened his walk as he saw me, he approached me with a calmer tone as he glanced to Ava, seeing she was giving him the cold shoulder as she questioned, "do you need something?",

the guys swiftly said, "have you seen a cat with yellow eyes, I know this is weird, but I saw this when I was close to death, you must of seen it too Martha",

I frowned a little, unnerved to how he knew my name, I've not gone to him for anything, this was getting weird, maybe Ava was right to not talk to him.

I said with caution, "I don't know how you know my name, but-",
"I saw it on the local newspaper,the guy got charge and arrested", the guy said firmly, he seemed to want to make sure he wasn't; weird, I still felt weird talking to him, especially with the cat thing.
I glanced to the hospital, recalling it ran inside, curiously I wondered, "you said about this lady, that she's in there, why do you need to talk to her? You don't seem to know her",
Ava interrupted, "we don't need to be feeding this, can we go, please?",
her eyes wondered to the man, seeing he was stubborn and wasn't going to budge until I told him what he wanted.
The guy said quickly, "just tell me, did you see the cat, I saw it, the lady was scared of it, she said it was going to kill her",
Carter may have seen it too, maybe that's why the cats in there, the jobs not done. I'm starting to not trust what I see anymore, maybe the cat was trying to kill me.
All the speculations couldn't prove its motive yet, but I did see it, the least I can tell him is I saw it.
With slight hesitance I stated, "okay I saw it, is that all you need to hear?",
Ava looked annoyed but kept it to herself as

the guy said softly, "yeah, thanks",
he left quickly, leaving us to to again, be at another bickering session.
She was always defensive with me, maybe she's protective of me, but I can look after myself, if there's not a car involved that is, that wasn't a fair fight.

Chapter Ten
Ominous

They stray from me, without the help I would of gotten to them sooner.
My objective is simple, kill, I don't guide them to death, I am death.
We hold many kinds of forms, some know what to do, and some pity the living and spare them, I don't my life is not worth splitting to ensure the life stays breathing.
One person is close, a small village in the middle of nowhere, and I hear more are following, it's going to be a good trip, they won't hear me arrive.
No one ever does.

Chapter Eleven
Kate

"I'm worried about you Gret",
he was by the table in the warehouse, he didn't invite me in, but I let myself in, he's been quite about what he does at work, he does doesn't have a stable job anymore, he just obsesses about his daughter and his last work partner.
Gret said firmly, "there's nothing to worry about-",
I pointed to the table as I exclaimed, "nothing to worry about?! what will people say with this? When they see this they'll think you're going around stalking teenagers, the hell Gret.",
he calmly explained, "Martha saw the same thing as I did, she confirmed it. The lady that tried to burn this place down must have seen the same thing",

With a huff I said softly, "what do you think this is doing to you? What will this help you with?",

I could always get angry with him, but I loved him and I wanted to understand, not lose my rag.

He gradually said, "to find Misty, it makes sense to me",

I held my tongue, only to make a like quiver of my lip as I said gently, "Gret-",

he cut me off as he said firmly, "I know where she is, I found it out with the help of the police lady I've been speaking with",

a frown showed on my face as he picked up his keys for the quad bike, I stopped him as I insisted, "well let me drive at least, you've not slept since yesterday",

I put the keys from his hand, if he's going off on another episode at least I'm behind the wheel.

He lead the way to my car outside the yard, he noticed my BMW was all clean and tidy, he tried to lighten the situation as he said,

"we're going to have to go off road, hope you don't mind a bit of mud. The car looks nice",

I gave a slight smile, seeing I really just wanted him to not do this to himself, but maybe with someone there, he might be able to see things clearer.

He directed me as I drove, we passed his house, driving though the town where Misty would of went to her friends that night, this was getting worse, I think I know where he wanted to go, it was everywhere. Even with his work mate, his was more of bad timing than anything else, some gang crossed path with him, same thing happened to this poor teen that's now in hospital by the same gang.

My heart ached as we drove past to the country side, seeing the gloomy dark fields as it was midnight at this point, my goal was to try to get Gret home…now I'm off on a late drive, heading to break his heart even more than it is now.

We passed under this bridge, I heard about a lady that jumped from it, this place is all bad news.

Gret motioned, here, to the right there, he said eagerly, "the lady said I may find something there",

I slowly pulled over to the right, parking near an overgrown field that stretched far.

As I stopped the car and turned it off, I gave a huff before asking, "who is this woman? Why would she tell you where to go but not be here herself? Doesn't seem like a police thing to do",

He handed me his phone as he stated, "just find her on here and call her yourself, or call Memphis, he's helped me too",

Gret left the car, heading out into the field with a small pocket light, I was torn to what I should do, but I quickly scrolled his phone, there isn't any recent calls from anyone else, the last call was from me and that was today.

I looked outside, seeing Gret was further from the car, shit I really need to get him back home, this is torture.

As I got out the car, I kept his phone in my hand as I called, "Gret, where are you going?!",

I started following, trudging in mud as he yelled back, "Misty, she's out here somewhere",

my words were getting harder as I said loudly, "Misty? She's not going to be here Gret, I don't think this is going to help",

Gret ignored me and kept looking, trying to not give up I exposed,

"Memphis isn't real, neither is the police lady, Gret I think this is in your head",

we were far from another, the rain was picking up, this is going shit, but I can't let him be out here on his own.

Gret shouted back, "no, you're just saying that to make me give up",

with force I ordered, "Gret, just look at me!",
he stopped, only to face me as I went on with frustration, "if no one can make you see it then I will just have to tell you it again until you do",
I walked closer as he said stressed, "what do you mean?",
upon showing him the phone from a distance, I pointed, "there is no Memphis, there is no police women, it's your grief. There's no easy way to tell you this, but Misty is dead, she's dead.",
Gret was trying to piece his words, causing me to grow more upset as I said firmly, "she died here Gret, you went here because you already knew where she was. Her friends killed her at that party she went to, she was taken here",
He tried to stop me talking as he said in disbelief, "no, that can't be true",
With a strain to my voice I snapped, "it is Gret, her friends assaulted her and left her here to die, it was on the news, you saw it, I know you did",
gradually he walked towards me, seeing the phone as I handed it back to him, I took the torch as he went through his phone, seeing it was true, he had made the people up to cope with something he didn't want to accept, I

wouldn't want to accept it either, but we can't bring back the dead.

His eyes reddened with tears as he said solemnly, "I just want her back Kate, she's I had left",

I gently put my hands to his face, taking his tears away with my thumbs as I said softly, "you can't",

I didn't know what else to say, I can't say it will get better, I lost both my parents at a young age, and I know the pain, the desperation to find something to bring them back.

He started to sob, seeing I wasn't going to change my words, they weren't sweet, but they were true.

I brought him towards me, letting him just have a long hug, I didn't care how long we were out here for, I needed him to make that step today.

Acceptance is never easy.

Chapter Twelve
Ava

We were at my place, still talking about the guy she spoke to outside the hospital, I wished we could just stop the conversation already, but she was getting worked up over it. It gained to nearing midnight, but I was willing to talk it out until we reached some sort of solution at least.

I had a hot cup of coffee cupped within my hands, having my back to the counter as I said calmly, "so what if we all saw what he saw, what does it even mean?",

Martha refused to drink the tea I made her, leaving it to grow colder as she stated, "maybe it means danger, I don't know, the lady was scared of it though, so I don't think she saw what we did, maybe that's what the guy was thinking about",

we were going full loop again, okay I can't keep deflecting the question that it seems weird, but it just, doesn't make sense to me yet.
I glanced to my left, seeing my phone was going off, out talk stopped as I answered it, I said, "Carter? You okay?",
he quietly said, "I need you to come here, something feels weird",
I frowned as I looked to Martha, she was worried, so was I. Quickly I said, "we're on our way",
I hung the phone up, only to focus on Martha as I stressed, "I think maybe the cat is up to something, like you said, you saw it go in the hospital, could be up to anything",
we left the house with haste, getting into my car as I drove us back to the hospital.
I don't know if they're gonna allow late visitors, but I've been there that many times I know my way in.
Martha glanced to me as she said softly, "do you think that this cat thing we keep seeing, that it's trying to kill us, or something",
I gave a slight thought, only to sigh a little before saying, "I don't know, I can't make sense of it. I know I've seen it before, but I'm not sure what it wants, what it's trying to do",

even though I had a strong cup of coffee, my eyes were still heavy with tiredness, swear I kept seeing a sort of shadow go near the car, by the pathway.
I frowned more in focus, keeping us on track to the hospital as I said shortly, "I don't think they have night visitors here",
the hospital was shut, only allowing emergency stops here.
I parked the car further from the hospital, making sure I won't get a ticket for parking on the pathway a little, we had a bit of a walk to get into the hospital, but I'd rather that than be stopped before even entering.
As we left the car, the night was crisp, it was sharp as the wind passed us.
Martha wondered, "you said they're not having night visitors, how are we going to get in?",
With a smirk I said, "back door, they never have enough staff, so they don't check the back door",
she soon pointed, "they'll have cameras though, we can't avoid that",
I directed us to the left side of the hospital, seeing the grounds pass us as we curved to the back of the building.
Martha was still worried about the cameras, but I reassured, "it's fine, if we get caught, I

know what to say",
she let a smirk only to joke, "it's like you've done this before",
I could only let a small snuff to her joke, I couldn't tell her I've broken into here before, a few times to be honest.
The back gate had a pad lock on it, but it was a decoy, it was broken as I could slip the lock out of place without hassle.
Martha was curious as she said, "how did you know that lock would just, not work?",
I glanced back to here as admitted, "I used to be a drug addicted and I broke in here with a few friends, who are no longer with me",
she didn't know how to take the sudden news, or even know what to say first, but I let a slight smile as is said shortly, "come on, we got to go and see if Carter is in one piece",
when saying that the hospital lights were going weird, I know it's cold today, but perhaps too cold.
I let a sigh as I walked to the hospital, seeing we should pick up, maybe the power cut is freaking him out.
We hurried to the open grounds, passing the benches as we headed to the large glass double doors to the hospital.
The floor was shinning pale blue, the walls were a glossy white, making this more

unnerving as the lights would flicker off an on briefly.

I opened the door for us, the lock system wasn't working due from the power cut, maybe it was all in good timing, but I didn't like this. Seemed all too convenient.

Chapter Thirteen
Carter

The hospital was being weird, I couldn't handle it anymore, the lights going off and on, I did try to get a nurse but there was no hope in doing that with the bedside button, just didn't work with the faulty power.

I sat on the edge of the, grumbling a little as my stab wounds were still piercing with pain.

I looked to the drip I was attached to, it didn't seem to be working so well, this was turning crap.

Without much thought I ripped out the drips, standing myself with force as I needed to leave the room, find someone. A frown grew to my face as I approached the door, seeing a faint shadow pass the door.

As I left the room the hall stretched for both ways, it was creepy. Gradually I brought myself to call, "hello? Anyone here?", the silence in return was deafening, maybe I should just call Ava.

My phone slipped out of my hand when I went to take it out of my pocket, it was hard to grip as I crouched left, the pain was growing unbearable.

The lights started to flicker as I reached for it, to which my motion slowed, seeing two red dots across the room, the lights were turning off as it was passing under it.

Hastily I took my phone, forcing myself to get up as the stitches started to peel open, reopening my wounds as I stood up.

With panic I called Ava, limping away helplessly from the red eyes as I waited for her to pick up.

Ava soon answered, "we're on our way to you",

quickly I interrupted, "no, you'll get killed. I'm on the stairs to the front of the hospital",

"but we're to the back stairs, we're on the other side of the hospital, just don't move",

Ava replied like she knew what to do, but she doesn't know what I just saw, which is more reason I may have to face this stupid thing.

I glanced back at it, seeing the lights were still pitching to darkness, and the eyes only grew brighter and redder.

It showed more of itself as I stared at it, seeing it was a large snake, dark black scales with a purple tint to it.

My heart thumped heavily as it approached, causing me to drop my phone as I noticed my stomach was bleeding more.

Sounds started to distort as I knelt to the floor, feeling my shirt as the snake thing was going towards me.

It made loud hisses, ringing my ears, making me feel nauseous as it went face to face with. Watching me with a blank look, but the eyes showed hunger. It's teeth dripped with black liquid, it didn't stain the floor it pattered upon, it was weird, it was like something stopped it from getting closer.

A noise interrupted its hissing, forcing it to look behind as the orange eyes trailed behind it, not the same one I saw from the attack, but it was a cat.

It hissed at the snake, stopping it from getting closer as my heart was staring to thump to a less deafening tone, my breaths calmed seeing the snake was leaving me. The cat made loud meows, it started to grew unbearable as it shrieked to the snakes movements.

I had my hands over my ears as it echoed in the hall, only to soon be startled as hands grasped my shoulders.

The hall was no longer dark, and I could see a nurse ahead of me, she said firmly, "he's going to bleed out, we need him back in his room",

I got up, only to slur, "I was trying to find a nurse, I couldn't find anyone, the button wasn't working",

the brown haired man gave a slight nod only to reassure, "we're having a power issue at the moment, but we'll have someone close by, the morning team are here",

as we walked down the hall, back to my room, I looked at the floor I passed, seeing no snake there, nor the cat, it would be crazy for me to mention this to anyone that wasn't Ava or Martha.

I went back into the room, the nurse got a doctor to patch me up again, it was still weird I couldn't find a nurse until this point, maybe they are understaffed here, but it was odd, it was like no one here…felt like it anyways.

Printed in Great Britain
by Amazon